Clifford's puppy days

THE BIG RED STOP SIGN

by Helen Delaney

Illustrated by Steve Haefele

Based on the Scholastic book series
"Clifford The Big Red Dog"
by Norman Bridwell

ISBN 0-439-87773-3

12 11 10 9 8 7 6 5 4 3 2 1   6 7 8 9 10/0

Designed by Michael Massen
Printed in the U.S.A.
First Printing, October 2006

SCHOLASTIC INC.

New York   Toronto   London   Auckland   Sydney
Mexico City   New Delhi   Hong Kong   Buenos Aires

"It's Saturday morning, Clifford!"

shouted Emily Elizabeth.

"No school today!"

Clifford wagged his tail.

Clifford and Emily Elizabeth

could play all day long!

Clifford and Emily Elizabeth ate
breakfast quickly.

"More eggs?" asked Mr. Howard.

"No time, Dad,"

Emily Elizabeth answered.

"I'm taking Clifford for a walk!"

"Ready to go?" Mrs. Howard asked.

"Remember, safety first."

"Don't worry, Mom," Emily Elizabeth said.
Clifford couldn't wait to get outside and
have fun!

The bright sun felt warm
on Clifford's fur.
The spring breeze smelled sweet.
What a day for a walk!

"Wait, Clifford!"

Emily Elizabeth called.

Hurry up, Emily Elizabeth!

Clifford thought.

HONK HONK!

A loud horn startled the tiny red puppy!

He stumbled backward as a bus

zoomed by.

"Look out!" a lady on a bike

shouted.

"A puppy like you could get hurt!"

Emily Elizabeth hugged Clifford tight.

Clifford's heart beat fast.

"Clifford!" Emily Elizabeth said.

"That wasn't safe!"

What did I do wrong? Clifford wondered.

"Let's stay in the playground,
far from the busy street,"
Emily Elizabeth said sadly.

But what about our walk?
Clifford thought.

"Did you see the big red sign?"

Norville chirped.

"What does it mean?"

Clifford asked him.

"It says FLY!" Norville answered.

"Fly up high above the cars!"

Clifford had to try it!

Clifford ran to the big red sign.

"Where are you going now?"

Emily Elizabeth called.

Watch this! Clifford thought.

Clifford jumped up into the air.

"Fly, Clifford, fly!" Norville cried.

Clifford didn't fly.

He landed.

THUMP!

"Silly puppy," Emily Elizabeth said.

"That big red sign means STOP!"

"Oops," Norville whispered.
"I guess it's a FLY sign only
for birds!"

"I have a lot to teach you, puppy,"

Emily Elizabeth said.

"Let's practice safety so we can take our walk."

"*WOOF!*" Clifford agreed.

Clifford learned to always stay close
to Emily Elizabeth.

And to always wait at the big red stop sign before crossing the street.

Look left, then right, then left again.

Are there cars coming?

Always make sure it's safe

to cross the street.

Always stay on the sidewalk.

"The sidewalk is for us, Clifford,"

Emily Elizabeth said.

"The street is for traffic."

"You're doing great!"

Emily Elizabeth told Clifford.

He felt proud to follow the rules.

Clifford felt very important.

He kept close to Emily Elizabeth,

and they walked safely back home.

"How was your walk?"

Mr. Howard asked.

"They kept an eye on each other,"

Mrs. Howard answered.

"We're good walkers!" laughed Emily Elizabeth.

"Safety first, right, Clifford?"

"*Woof!*" Clifford barked happily.

He had a wonderful day, but it was good to be home.

Circle the right answer.

1. What did Emily Elizabeth and Clifford want to do on Saturday?

   a. Play baseball

   b. Take a walk

   c. Bake a cake

2. What did Norville say that the STOP sign meant?

   a. Walk

   b. Stop

   c. Fly

Which happened first?

Which happened next?

Which happened last?

Write a 1, 2, or 3 in the space after each sentence.

Clifford learned safety rules. _____

Clifford and Emily Elizabeth ate breakfast. _____

Clifford and Emily Elizabeth start their walk. _____

Answers:

Clifford and Emily Elizabeth start their walk. (2)

Clifford and Emily Elizabeth ate breakfast. (1)

Clifford learned safety rules. (3)

2. c

1. b